Published by Scholastic Inc.,
90 Old Sherman Turnpike, Danbury, Connecticut 06816.

For information regarding permission, write to:
Disney Licensed Publishing,
114 Fifth Avenue, New York, New York 10011.

0-7172-7744-5

Printed in the U.S.A.
First printing, June 2005

Disney

Pooh's Heffalump MOVIE

SCHOLASTIC INC.

New York Toronto London Auckland Sydney
Mexico City New Delhi Hong Kong Buenos Aires

It had been so nice and summery in the Hundred-Acre Wood. But all that changed one morning. Little Roo was sleeping soundly when he was suddenly awakened by a strange trumpeting sound.

TA-ROOOT!

"What happened?" wondered Roo, looking out of his window. Outside, Pooh ran past carrying a honeypot. A panicked Piglet followed, holding a sheet. Then Tigger bounced by with a painting around his neck!

"Where's everybody going?" called Roo.

"To Rabbit's house," answered Piglet. "He'll know what to do!"

Roo waved good-bye to his mother, Kanga.
Then he hurried over to Rabbit's house, too.

"What's all this about?" asked a sleepy Rabbit
when he answered the door. His friends explained
how the strange trumpeting sound had frightened
them all. Pooh had fallen into a honeypot, Piglet
had run into his clothesline, and a picture had come
crashing down on Tigger.

Then Roo
discovered a huge
footprint.

"What sort of
creature, do you
suppose, would be
attached to a foot that
big?" asked Pooh. "There's only one
thing it could be—a heffalump!" declared Rabbit.

Everyone except Roo gasped.

"What's a heffalump?" asked Roo.

"It's got horns and a spiky tail," Tigger told him.

"They're hazardous," agreed Rabbit. None of
them had ever seen a heffalump, but everyone knew
they were terrible creatures.

"And they live right over there in Heffalump
Hollow," added Rabbit.

Rabbit announced that they should go on an expedition to capture the heffalump. So everyone gathered their heffalump-hunting equipment.

But Rabbit thought catching heffalumps was for grown-ups and was too dangerous for Roo to go. "I'm sorry, Roo," Rabbit said softly.

Roo wished he was a grown-up so that he could go and catch a heffalump, too.

The next morning, the heffalump hunters set out. Soon they reached the fence that separated the Hundred-Acre Wood from Heffalump Hollow.

"Now remember everyone," said Rabbit, "the important thing is that we stick together!"

One by one the heffalump hunters flopped over the fence—except for Eeyore. "Don't let me hold you up," he called after his friends.

Determined to prove his bravery, Roo decided to catch a heffalump on his own. He grabbed his rope and hopped into Heffalump Hollow. But as he made his way through the forest, he thought someone— or something—was following him!

Roo kept walking. The sound got closer and closer. Then Roo felt something tap his shoulder! "Aaaahh!" screamed Roo.

"You're it!" a voice said. "Now you've got to catch me!"

Roo could only see a shadow in the darkness.

"Don't you want to play?" asked the voice.

"No," said Roo. "I've got to catch a heffalump."

Suddenly a cute little elephant-like creature rushed out of the darkness and rolled right into Roo. "You can catch me!" said the creature. "My name is Lumpy, and I'm a heffalump!"

Roo had heard how scary heffalumps were, but this fellow looked perfectly friendly. "Are you sure you are a heffalump?" asked Roo.

"My mum says I am." Lumpy giggled.

"If you are a heffalump, then where are your horns and spiky tail?" wondered Roo.

Lumpy shrugged. "A spiky tail? Wish I had one."

"If you are a heffalump, then . . . I'm capturing you!"
cried Roo, lassoing Lumpy.

But Lumpy just scampered off, pulling Roo along.

"Stop!" shouted Roo. "You've got to come with me
because . . . I'm a grown-up."

"A grown-up," Lumpy repeated. "You must have your own call then."

"My call?" Roo was confused.

"Like this," explained Lumpy. Then he lifted his trunk and tried to trumpet, but all that came out were a few small wheezes.

Suddenly they heard trumpeting.

"Got to go now," said Lumpy. "My mum is calling."

"Don't go yet. Let's go to see my friends first," said Roo.

"I don't know. . . ." Lumpy hesitated.

"Ple-e-ease," begged Roo.

"Well, okay," agreed Lumpy, and they headed back towards the Hundred-Acre Wood.

Meanwhile, Tigger and Rabbit were hiding in some bushes. Rabbit tried to lure the heffalump with his heffalump call, "*Brurrooo. Brurrooo.*"

The call echoed through the woods. "Oh, my what a dreadful sound!" Piglet said with a shiver.

Bravely, Pooh and Piglet crept towards the sound.

"Do you see it?" asked Piglet.

"I see a tail," whispered Pooh.

"Are there horns, too?" Piglet asked.

"Two of them," answered Pooh.

The two friends
pounced. "In the name of
the Hundred-Acre Wood,"
Pooh and Piglet proudly
announced, "we capture
you!" Then they examined
their catch.

"Pooh, have you
noticed that heffalumps
look a lot like Rabbits?"
asked Piglet.

"And why do you
think that is, Piglet?"
said Rabbit, fuming.

"Oh, d-d-dear, the
heffalump knows my
name!" gasped Piglet.

Pooh looked at
his trap. "Hello, Tigger,"
Pooh said innocently.
"Did you happen to
see the heffalump
I just captured?"

Back at the fence that separated Heffalump
Hollow and the Hundred-Acre Wood, Lumpy
hesitated. "I'm not supposed to go over there,"
said Lumpy. "Scary things live there. There's a
stripey thing that bounces."

"That's Tigger," explained Roo.

"And there's this little pink monster that
squeals and shakes," continued Lumpy.

"You're wrong about Piglet. He wouldn't hurt
a fly," promised Roo. "My friends aren't scary."

"There's nothing scary here," Roo told Lumpy.

"Promise?" Lumpy asked softly.

"Promise!" Roo answered.

With that, and a little help from Roo, Lumpy squished through the fence into the Hundred-Acre Wood.

Soon Lumpy and Roo arrived at Pooh's house.

"Hmm, it looks like nobody's home," said Roo, peeking inside.

The smell of honey caught Lumpy's attention. It was his snack time, after all.

"Wait! That's Pooh's honey," Roo cried as Lumpy poured some into his mouth. Then Roo shrugged. "Oh, well, I guess he won't mind."

Lumpy and Roo didn't mean to, but they made a bit of a mess out of Pooh's house.

Then they went over to Rabbit's house, but Rabbit wasn't home either. And Lumpy couldn't help munching on the watermelon in Rabbit's garden.

"They must still be out on the expedition," said Roo about his missing friends.

Just for fun, Roo spat a watermelon seed at Lumpy.

Lumpy giggled. "Oh yeah." He inhaled a whole watermelon and then spat the seeds back at Roo. *Rat-a-tat-tat!*

Soon the two were having a big fun food fight!

Again, Lumpy and Roo didn't mean to, but they made a bit of a mess of Rabbit's garden. And they were quite a mess, too.

"My mum is not going to like this," said Lumpy, looking at himself.

Roo thought of his mama. "We had better get cleaned up," Roo agreed. He knew just what to do.

Roo led Lumpy to a large pond. "Cannonball!" yelled Roo, jumping in.

Lumpy laughed and jumped in, too.

The new friends had a wonderful time in the water.

Then Lumpy heard his mother's call again. It was time to go. Roo removed the rope from Lumpy's neck and tossed it away.

"Lumpy," said Roo quietly, "you're not captured anymore."

The friends smiled at each other. Then they headed back into Heffalump Hollow so Lumpy could find his mother.

Meanwhile, the heffalump hunters had finally returned to the Hundred-Acre Wood. "All in all, it was a successful heffalump expedition," declared Rabbit. "Just look around! You don't see any heffalumps, do you?"

Then Rabbit spotted heffalump tracks—leading straight to Pooh's house.

Inside Pooh's house, the gang found broken honeypots everywhere.

Pooh sighed. "Oh bother. I don't think our heffalump expedition is successful anymore."

"Rabbit!" Tigger shouted frantically when they arrived at Rabbit's house.

Rabbit looked in horror at his ruined garden. "The heffalumps are among us!" screamed Rabbit.

"It's an invasion!" shouted Tigger.

"We're trapped!" cried Piglet.

"That's it!" Rabbit said suddenly. "We need traps!"

So everyone got to work building traps to catch the heffalump. Piglet dug a deep hole and covered it with branches. Pooh made a cage out of sticks and put a not-quite-empty honeypot in it as bait.

"Behold!" cried Tigger proudly as he showed
off his net trap. "A super-duper-extralooper,
hunka hunka heffa-trap!"

"Now," said Rabbit when all the traps were
finished, "to await the attack!"

Just then Kanga came hopping along. "Have
any of you seen Roo?" she asked. "He should
have been home by now."

But no one had seen Roo all day.

Back in Heffalump Hollow, Roo and Lumpy heard Lumpy's mother trumpeting again.

"I really have to go," said Lumpy anxiously. "She sounds worried."

"I'll help you find her," said Roo.

They wandered through the forest, searching everywhere. But they couldn't find Lumpy's mother. Lumpy tried to call her; but instead of a trumpet sound, only a weak wheeze came out.

"Missusses Heffaaalummpp" Roo called. Still, the friends couldn't find her.

After a while Lumpy sniffed. "We haven't heard my mum in a really long time." The little heffalump sat down.

Roo tried to comfort his friend, but he couldn't. "I want my mum," Lumpy said softly.

"Me, too," said Roo. "Wait! My mom! She'll know what to do! Come on!" So the two headed back to the Hundred-Acre Wood.

It wasn't long before they found Kanga and all of
Roo's friends. But when Rabbit and the gang saw Roo
with a heffalump, they panicked.

"He's got Roo!" Rabbit screamed frantically. They
charged towards the heffalump before Roo could explain.

Lumpy raced into the forest to try and get away.

"No! Wait!" cried Roo.

"This is Lumpy."

Roo raced after Lumpy and finally found him caught in one of the traps. Lumpy was crying.

"You said they wouldn't be scary," Lumpy sniffed. "You promised."

Roo felt like crying, too. "I'm so sorry." Then Roo climbed on top of the cage and unfastened the ropes that held it together, setting Lumpy free.

From the bushes, Kanga had seen it all. She was happy that her son had stood by his new friend.

At that moment the heffalump hunters arrived.
They saw Lumpy hugging Roo and thought they
had to save Roo.

"Drop my little bouncing buddy, you heffaly-
rascalump!" cried Tigger.

The gang surrounded poor, terrified Lumpy.

"Leave him alone!" pleaded Roo. "You're scaring him."

Kanga jumped in front of Rabbit and the others.
"What on earth are you all doing?" she demanded.
   "We're rescuing Roo from the heffalump," said Rabbit.
   "We were wrong about heffalumps," protested Roo.
"They're not scary creatures. He's just like us. Lumpy is my
friend," Roo added. "So they have to uncapture him."

But Lumpy was still scared, and he lost his
footing as he backed up on the steep slope.

"Lumpy!" cried Roo, grabbing a rope. Lumpy
managed to gain his footing on his own, but Roo
went flying through the air! "Aaaahh!" Roo cried.
Little Roo landed in a huge pile of dead trees at
the bottom of the steep slope.

"Roo!" cried Kanga. The Hundred-Acre Wood
friends tried to rescue him. But they couldn't
reach him, and the trees were too heavy to move.

"Hold on, Roo," called Lumpy. He knew just what to do.

Lumpy ran to the edge of the forest, lifted his trunk, and blew as hard as he could. For the first time ever, he trumpeted! *TA-ROOOT!*

He had finally found his heffalump call, just when it was needed most.

Hearing her son's call, Mama Heffalump trumpeted
back loudly and came crashing out of the forest. She
was relieved Lumpy was safe.

"I'm okay, Mum, but my friend Roo is in trouble,"
Lumpy told her.

Lumpy led his mother to the edge of the steep slope.
With ease, Mama Heffalump moved some of the logs where
Roo was trapped. Then she carefully plucked out tiny Roo
with her trunk and gently passed him to Kanga.

"She did it!" cried Lumpy proudly.

"Oh, Roo," said Kanga, hugging Roo tightly.

The gang from the
Hundred-Acre Wood realized
they were wrong about
heffalumps. Rabbit and the
others apologized to Lumpy.

"Lumpy, sweetheart, we really should be going," said Mama Heffalump.

"Could we please stay just a bit longer?" asked Lumpy.

"Ple-e-ease," added Roo.

"Well, I don't see why not." Mama Heffalump chuckled.

"I suppose so," agreed Kanga.

Mama Heffalump wrapped her trunk around Kanga, and the friends jumped for joy.

"Forward, bounce," Lumpy called. And off the two friends went, laughing all the way.

EYE SPY

Take your own expedition into Heffalump Hollow. Look back in the story and try to find these pictures.